The Urbana Free Library

To renew: call 217-367-4057
or go to "*urbanafreelibrary.org*"
and select "Renew/Request Items"

A Christmas Spider's Miracle

By Trinka Hakes Noble

Illustrated by Stephen Costanza

10/11
16 95

For Ruby and Ivy

With my love,

T.H.N.

For Sue and Mike with love,

S.C.

Sleeping Bear Press
315 E. Eisenhower Parkway, Suite 200
Ann Arbor, MI 48108
www.sleepingbearpress.com

Sleeping Bear Press is an imprint of Gale, a part of Cengage Learning.

10 9 8 7 6 5 4 3 2 1

Printed by China Translation & Printing Services Limited,Guangdong
Province,China. 1st printing.   04/2011

Library of Congress Cataloging-in-Publication Data

Noble, Trinka Hakes.
A Christmas spider's miracle / written by Trinka Hakes Noble ;
illustrated by Stephen Costanza.
p. cm.
Summary: A poor peasant woman who has no money for gifts or a
special meal for her children gets help from a kindly mother spider
on Christmas.
ISBN 978-1-58536-602-6 (alk. paper)
[1. Folklore—Ukraine.] I. Costanza, Stephen, ill. II. Title.
PZ8.1.N698Ch 2011
398.2--dc22
[E]   2010038185

Author's Note

One of my fondest Michigan childhood memories is trudging through deep snow into the woods with my brothers and sisters each December to find the perfect tree for Christmas. It had to be a red cedar because my mother loved how it filled our little farmhouse with its rich scent. It was a good thing my father was a patient man because it took us some time to find a tree that was just right. And when we did, we instinctively formed a circle around it while my father cut it down. Sometimes there would be a small bird's nest in our tree which we always left as part of our decorations. And once, much to our delight, a couple of moths hatched out.

So, when I first heard of this old Ukrainian tale, it made perfect sense to me that a spider could be carried into a warm house on a freshly cut tree and begin to spin. Further research uncovered a very special spider called the nursery spider that actually spins other things besides webs, like warm little pockets for her spiderlings. Although there are several versions of this old tale, my country childhood inspired me to spin and weave my own story.

Long ago, in the land of old Ukraine, there once was a winter so
bleak and so cold that the peasant folk feared it might never end.
The little villages and farms shivered under a frozen mantle of deep
snow. The pale sun made little difference as the cold nights grew
longer and longer.

Folks could barely wait until Christmas Eve, that long cold night
when everyone would light candles to fill the darkness with
hope. Oh how they'd feast and dance and make such
merriment to celebrate the coming of Christmas, for
it was only then that the sun would return to
lengthen and warm the coming days.

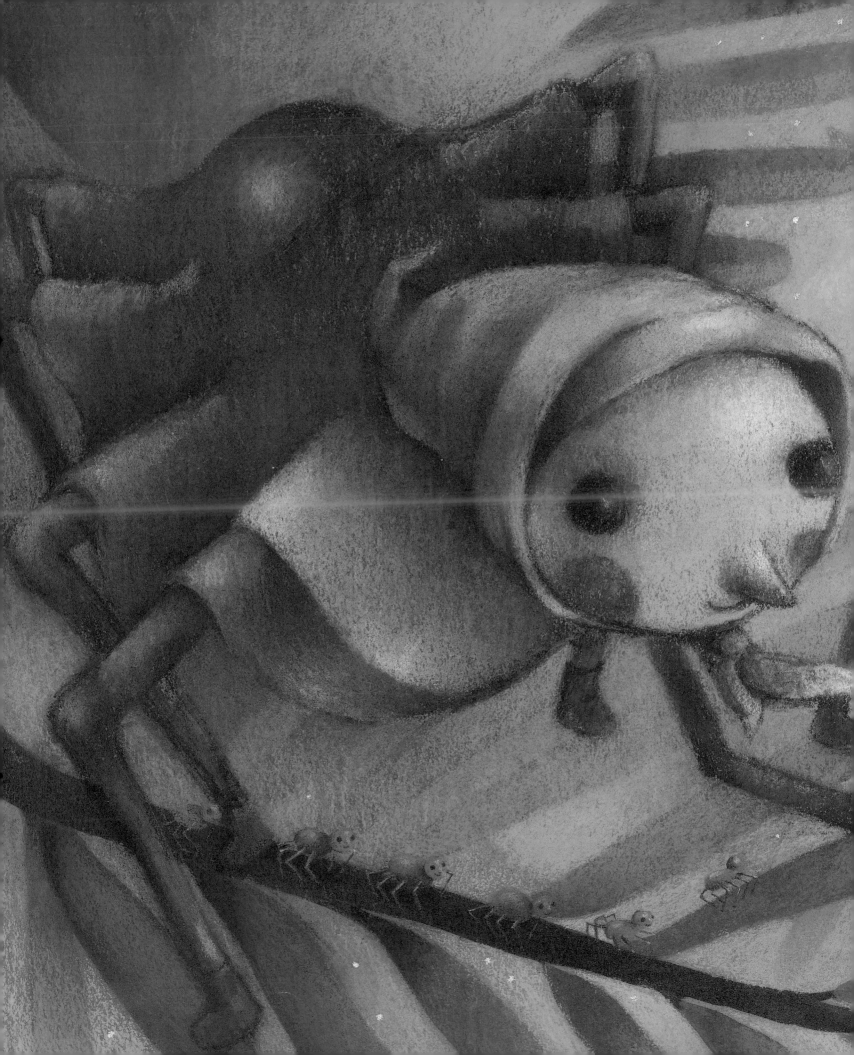

At the edge of the forest, in this bleakest of winters, there lived a mother spider who knew nothing of Christmas. She had set up housekeeping with her children in a small fir tree, for she did not think it safe to live in a house.

People did not take kindly to spiders, though she did not understand why. Spiders rid houses of pests, like flies and moths. But, alas, that was the way of things, so mother spider did her best to weave her webs and feed her children.

Soon it was the day before Christmas and, as the dark afternoon waned into dusk, promising an even colder night, mother spider became worried. With great care, she spun warm little pockets for each tiny spider and tucked them in.

"Now sleep, my little ones," she whispered. "I'll keep watch over you."

But, as mother spider wrapped her eight slender legs around her children, she feared she might not survive this long night. Soon the piercing cold overtook her and she descended into a deep, silent sleep.

Nearby, in a tumbledown cottage, there lived another mother and her children. The poor peasant woman earned what she could by mending and darning other people's clothes, but there never was anything left over, certainly nothing for Christmas. Now Christmas Eve was almost here.

At dusk the Christmas Market was crowded with shoppers as the poor mother crossed the village square to deliver her mending. Festive stalls were overflowing with Christmas wares.

Brightly colored toys and twinkling trinkets filled one. Warm woolly mittens and snug embroidered scarves hung in another. Spiced cakes, braided breads, and honeyed goods were stacked high. Shiny decorations and sparkling tree ornaments were everywhere.

Musicians played, acrobats tumbled, puppeteers performed, and jugglers juggled while the waxy glow of candles warmed the bitterly cold night.

The crisp pine-scented air made folks giddy. Merrily they hurried and scurried, to and fro, gathering everything for Christmas.

But the poor mother could buy nothing. No gay hair ribbons nor warm woolly mittens. No honeyed things. Not a sprig of greenery nor the smallest toy. Not even the tiniest ornament nor the thinnest strip of tinsel. No, not one little bit of Christmas could she buy for her children.

The only thing she could afford was one spool
of thread for mending and a meager soup bone.
There was nothing for the woman to do but
return home empty handed.

But when the mother opened the door, her children were rosy with excitement.

"Come, dear Mother. Seat thyself," they cried, prancing and dancing about her. Then, with great fanfare, the children placed a steaming bowl of watery turnip gruel before their mother, for it was all they had.

The mother clapped her hands with joy. "Oh, my dear little ones! You remembered!" For it was the custom throughout the land for children to bring their parents a dish of food as a treat on Christmas Eve.

She closed her eyes, breathed in the wispy vapors, and took a small sip. The thin turnip gruel warmed her heart and nourished her soul, for it was made by the little hands of her dear children.

"Oh my, this is delicious!" the mother exclaimed. "You all must taste it." Like hungry baby birds in a nest, each child eagerly waited as the mother spooned the gruel into their bowls.

"Mmmm…what a Christmas Eve feast," cooed the mother.

"Mmmm…yes…a feast," chirped the children, all smiling and rubbing their tummies.

That Christmas Eve, as the poor mother tucked her children into the thin quilt she'd sewn from scraps, she whispered, "Now sleep, my little ones. I'll keep watch over you."

But the mother's heart was breaking for she had nothing to give her good children on Christmas morning.

At the very least, she decided to fetch a small tree from the forest, even though she had nothing to decorate it with.

Outside the frozen mantle of snow glistened like a diamond-studded cape, its icy blue crystals reflecting the silent shimmering stars above. All was hushed. There wasn't a sound, not a stirring of any kind. The whole world was silent and still, waiting for Christmas.

The peasant woman stepped lightly across the frozen crust. Soon she saw a small fir tree at the edge of the forest. "How perfect," she whispered, and took the little tree home.

She placed the small fir tree in the window where her children would see it when they awoke. Then she sat at her sewing table and drew patterns of the ornaments she'd seen in the Christmas Market: a golden star, a shepherd's hook, a silver bell, a gossamer angel, a crystal snowflake, and a dancing elf. But with only mismatched bits and pieces, frayed odds and ends, a broken button, and snippets of old thread, she couldn't fashion a one.

Overwhelmed with sadness, the mother laid her head on the table and slipped into a troublesome slumber.

Even though the humble cottage was cold, it was still warmer than the forest. Mother spider began to stir, then yawned and stretched her eight slender legs. Suddenly, with great alarm, she realized she was in a house!

Her first thought was to gather her little spiderlings and flee, but when she saw the children sweetly nestled together under the thin quilt of scraps, her fear vanished. She dropped down for a closer look.

Being an expert weaver and spinner herself, she couldn't help but admire the fine stitching, the masterful darning of each hole, and the exquisite mending of every tear. And, being a mother herself, she couldn't help but cover an exposed toe, slip a nightcap over a tiny ear, and tug the thin quilt up under a little chin.

Mother spider felt a kinship to the sleeping peasant woman. "We are the same," she whispered, "two mothers trying to keep our children warm on this cold, cold night. You have saved me and mine from freezing. Perhaps I can repay your kindness."

With a true artist's sense of design
and an expert knowledge of all things
woven and spun, the mother spider studied the
peasant woman's drawings and patterns. She examined
the bits of thread, the broken button, and the frayed snippets.
Then gathering everything, she scurried back to the little fir tree.

Suddenly, in the corner of the window, a fluttering moth caught her eye.

"Oh my," sighed mother spider, "the last thing this poor woman needs is
more moth holes to mend." Quickly, she dispatched the moth, wrapped
it up for tomorrow's dinner, then set to her spinning.

On that night of nights, that Christmas Eve so very long ago, one busy little spider darted back and forth, over and under, in and out, around and through, up and down, to and fro, hurrying and scurrying, silently weaving and spinning by soft starlight.

Above the starry heavens shone down on one tumbledown cottage, silently keeping watch over all who dwelt within.

On that long-ago Christmas Day, the morning sun rose strong and bright through the window. With each ray of sunlight the spider's spinnings and weavings began to shimmer and glimmer like a tapestry of gold and silver. A humble mother and her children stood in silent wonderment at the miraculous sight before them.

First a shepherd's hook appeared with a bit of red thread. Then a silvery bell began to shine. Above it a delicate silken angel floated. Next a snowflake, woven with bits of white thread, sparkled like crystal while a merry elf danced with half a button for a hat. And finally, a radiant golden star shone atop the tree like a crown.

As her children's eyes gleamed, the mother's eyes tearfully glistened.

This was Christmas.

Christmas was here.

That Christmas Day, one family feasted on thin turnip gruel flavored with a meager soup bone, while the other dined on moth. But both mothers felt richly blessed; one by the safety of a warm house and the other by a small spider's Christmas miracle.

Even to this day, in the land of Ukraine, if you see a spider on Christmas Day, it will bring you good fortune for the whole year. But just to be sure, Christmas trees across the land all have one very special ornament … a sparkling jeweled spider.